For Jamie
H.Z.

With love to Mae
K.G.

Text copyright © 1988 by Harriet Ziefert
Illustrations copyright © 1988 by Karen Gundersheimer
All rights reserved. Printed in Singapore for Harriet Ziefert, Inc.
First published in the U.S.A. in 1988 by Harper & Row, Publishers, Inc.,
10 East 53rd Street, New York, NY 10022. Published simultaneously
in Canada by Fitzhenry & Whiteside Limited, Toronto

Library of Congress Cataloging-in-Publication Data
Ziefert, Harriet.
  Me too! me too!

  Summary: Molly and her little sister have fun
playing indoors and outdoors on a rainy day
  [1. Play—Fiction.   2. Sisters—Fiction]
I. Gundersheimer, Karen, ill.   II. Title.
PZ7.Z487Me   [E]   87-11937
ISBN 0-06-026880-8
ISBN 0-06-026893-X (lib. bdg.)

ME TOO! ME TOO!

BY HARRIET ZIEFERT
ILLUSTRATED BY
KAREN GUNDERSHEIMER

R XZ

003

Harper & Row, Publishers

I'm Molly.
Jenny's my little sister.
It's raining hard outside,
so we are inside playing dress-up.

I put on mommy's skirt.
I put on daddy's hat and tie.

"Me too!" says Jenny.

I put on a fancy hat
and high-heeled shoes.

"Me too!" says Jenny.

I find clown pants
and furry slippers.

"Me too!" says Jenny.

It's still raining.
But only a little.
I'm tired of being inside,
so I say, "Jenny, let's ask Mommy
if we can play in the rain."

Mommy says we may go out
if we put on raincoats,
and rainhats, and rubber boots.

So we put on our rain clothes.
All of them.

I like the rain.

Jenny likes to feel raindrops on her cheeks.

When I catch raindrops,
Jenny says, "Me too!"

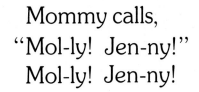

Mommy calls,
"Mol-ly! Jen-ny!"
Mol-ly! Jen-ny!

We jump in puddles.
I splash Jenny.
Jenny splashes me back.

When I taste the rain,
Jenny says, "Me too!"

I race Jenny to the house.

"Guess what I have for you
to take out in the rain?"
Mommy asks.

"Umbrellas!" we answer together.

We dance and twirl with our umbrellas.

"Me too! Me too!" says Mommy.